Cops and Robbers

Janet & Allan Ahlberg

PUFFIN

Ho Ho for the robbers
The cops and the robbers Ho Ho!

Here are the cops of London town,
Hardworking, brave and true.
They drink their tea,
Stay up till three
And take good care of you.

Here are the robbers of London town
With crowbars and skeleton keys.
They prowl and creep
When you're asleep
And take . . . whatever they please.

Ho Ho for the robbers
The cops and the robbers Ho Ho!

The worst of the robbers, as most of us know,
Is dreadful Grabber Dan.
His voice is gruff
And he's pinched enough stuff
To fill a furniture van.

His mates in the gang are Snatcher Jack
And baby-faced Billy-the-Bag;
Peg-leg Horace,
Fingers Maurice
And villainous Grandma Swagg.

Ho Ho for the robbers
The cops and the robbers Ho Ho!

Grabber Dan

Snatcher Jack

Billy-the-Bag

Peg-leg Horace

Fingers Maurice

Grandma Swagg

This dreadful, snatching, pilfering bunch
Would rob a baby of his lunch.

This sneaking, creeping, fingering lot
Would burgle a burglar, like as not.

This peg-legged, baby-faced, villainous crew
Would pick the pocket of a kangaroo.

Now, we hear, there's worse to come,
For the robbers are planning – the scalliwag scum –
To make a haul on Christmas Eve
Of all the toys that they can thieve.
Like crooked santas they'll creep about,
Pinching presents – not giving them out.

Ho Ho for the robbers
The cops and the robbers Ho Ho!

The best of the cops, by common consent,
Is upstanding Officer Pugh.
He can run like a hare
And fight like a bear;
And he's good at crosswords too.

So on Christmas Eve when the trouble began
The station sergeant said,
'The thing to do
Is to send for Pugh,
He'll get 'em – alive or dead!'

'Listen Pugh,' said the sergeant, 'the problem is this,
There are toys going missing galore.
From the size of the job,
We suspect it's a mob.
What they need's the strong arm of the Law!'

Ho Ho for the robbers
The cops and the robbers Ho Ho!

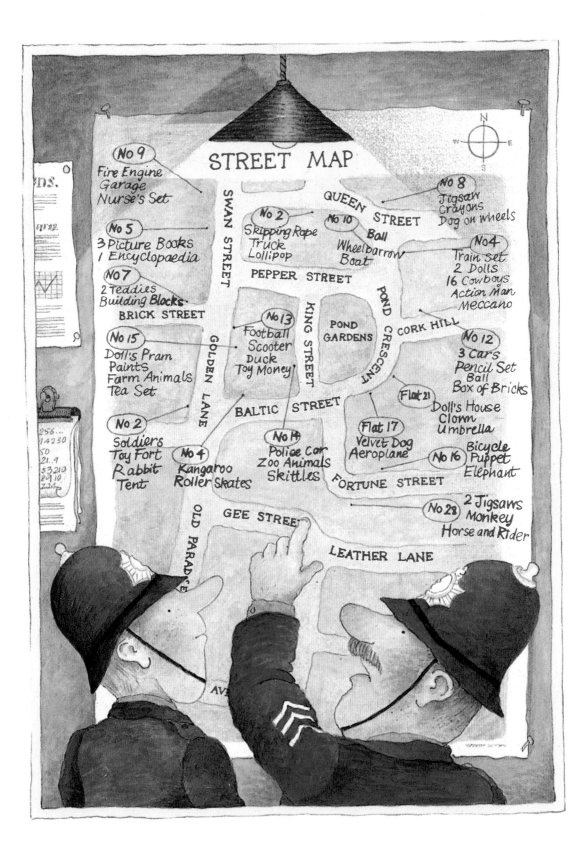

Meanwhile outside in the gloomy street
The strong arm of the robbers was working a treat,
And the strong leg too and the beady eye
Keeping watch for passers-by.
In at the windows, in at the doors,
Down the chimneys, under the floors,
Through silent rooms the robbers crept
While in their beds the children slept,

Dreaming of Santa Claus and snow
And what they'd get from Uncle Joe.
They never knew that 'Uncle' Maurice
Was robbing them – and 'Uncle' Horace.

Ho Ho for the robbers
The cops and the robbers Ho Ho!

The look-out man was Snatcher Jack;
He stood in a doorway yawning.
But when Officer Pugh
Came into view,
Jack saw him and whistled a warning.

Grandma Swagg, when the warning came,
Was pushing a pram up the road.
It was piled high with loot
And stolen to boot,
A thoroughly villainous load.

'Hallo, hallo,' said Officer Pugh,
'Now then, what's going on here?'
'Not much, young man,'
Said the criminal gran,
'We're just having a robbery, dear.'

Ho Ho for the robbers
The cops and the robbers Ho Ho!

Before Officer Pugh could unravel this clue
The robbers were on him like beasts from a zoo.

They knocked off his helmet and rumpled his tie,
Trod on his truncheon, kicked mud in his eye,

Pulled his ears and tickled his feet,
Threw half of his clothes all over the street,

Punched and pummelled him – Wham – Bam – SLAM
Even ran over him with the pram.

'Give up, give up!' the robbers cried
As they sat on the officer side by side.
'We've got you out-numbered five to one.'
(For in the confusion, Grandma had gone.)
But Officer Pugh just shook his head.
'We've hardly started, boys,' he said,
And he laughed a laugh and grinned a grin.
'Sitting comfortably are you? Then I'll begin!'

With a sudden leap he bounded free
And handcuffed Horace to a nearby tree;

Tied Maurice up in an empty sack
And beat the daylights out of Jack.

'Help!' shouted Billy. 'This can't be fair;
That Pugh's not human – he fights like a bear.
My mother was right – crime doesn't pay!'
And with these words he fainted away.

Grabber Dan was the last to cop it
(Grandma, of course, having chosen to hop it).
Dan tried to hide – the officer sought him.
Dan tried to run – the officer caught him.
Dan went to lift Pugh over his head.
The officer lifted Dan instead,
And whirled him round and swung him – WHOOSH!
Across the road and into a bush.

Down he tumbled, skidded, rolled;

Hit a concrete gnome and was knocked out cold.

Pugh dusted his hands and sat on the wall.

A little snow had begun to fall.

He looked at the gnome and patted its head.

'You could get a medal for this,' he said.

Ho Ho for the robbers

The cops and the robbers Ho Ho!

Here are the cops of London town
In the station at half-past two.
They drink their beer
And raise a cheer
For upstanding Officer Pugh.

Here are the robbers of London town
In cells all gloomy and grim.
'Let us out, let us out!
Not guilty!' they shout,
And, 'It wasn't me – it was him!'

Ho Ho for the robbers
The cops and the robbers Ho Ho!

And the toys? Oh, they were taken back
By a Santa Claus copper with a Santa Claus sack.
While the rest of the force searched day and night
For an elderly lady of medium height
With a fondness for earrings and red fox furs
And a habit of taking what wasn't hers.
She usually carried a sizeable bag;
Her name, of course, was Grandma Swagg.

Ho Ho for the robbers
The cops and the robbers Ho Ho!

PUFFIN BOOKS
Published by the Penguin Group:
London, New York, Australia, Canada, India, Ireland, New Zealand and South Africa
Penguin Books Ltd, Registered Offices: One Embassy Gardens, 8 Viaduct Gardens, London, SW11 7BW , England

puffinbooks.com

First published by William Heinemann Ltd 1978
Published by Puffin Books 1999
Reissued 2015
006

Made and printed in China

ISBN: 978–0–140–56584–3